EARLY BIRD STORIES

Dress-Up Day

All Kinds of Clothes

Lisa Bullard   Illustrated by Renée Kurilla

LERNER PUBLICATIONS ◆ MINNEAPOLIS

NOTE TO EDUCATORS

Find text recall questions at the end of each chapter. Critical-thinking and text feature questions are available on page 23. These help young readers learn to think critically about the topic by using the text, text features, and illustrations.

Lerner Publications Company
An imprint of Lerner Publishing Group, Inc.
241 First Avenue North
Minneapolis, MN 55401 USA

For reading levels and more information, look up this title at www.lernerbooks.com.

Photos on p. 22 used with permission of: FatCamera/Getty Images (kids playing soccer); monkeybusinessimages/Getty Images (kids in school); FatCamera/Getty Images (girls wearing hijabs).

Main body text set in Billy Infant.
Typeface provided by SparkyType.

Library of Congress Cataloging-in-Publication Data

Names: Bullard, Lisa, author. | Kurilla, Renée, illustrator.
Title: Dress-up day : all kinds of clothes / Lisa Bullard ; Illustrated by Renée Kurilla.
Description: Minneapolis : Lerner Publications, [2022] | Series: All kinds of people (early bird stories) | Includes bibliographical references and index. | Audience: Ages 5–8 | Audience: Grades K–1 | Summary: "Chloe is excited to pick out a special outfit for school, but she isn't sure of what to wear. Readers will learn how clothes can show a person's interests, personality, culture, and more!"— Provided by publisher.
Identifiers: LCCN 2021004106 (print) | LCCN 2021004107 (ebook) | ISBN 9781728436883 (library binding) | ISBN 9781728438573 (paperback) | ISBN 9781728438092 (ebook)
Subjects: LCSH: School children's clothing—Juvenile literature. | Readiness for school—Juvenile literature. | Clothing and dress—Juvenile literature.
Classification: LCC LB3024 .B85 2022 (print) | LCC LB3024 (ebook) | DDC 372.21—dc23

LC record available at https://lccn.loc.gov/2021004106
LC ebook record available at https://lccn.loc.gov/2021004107

Manufactured in the United States of America
1-49649-49577-4/13/2021

TABLE OF CONTENTS

CHAPTER 1
WHAT CLOTHES TELL US

I'm Chloe. It's dress-up day at school tomorrow. That means **no school uniform**!

Maybe I'll wear my karate uniform or dress as a firefighter. I love karate and want to be a firefighter when I'm older.

"Clothes say something about us," Mama says.

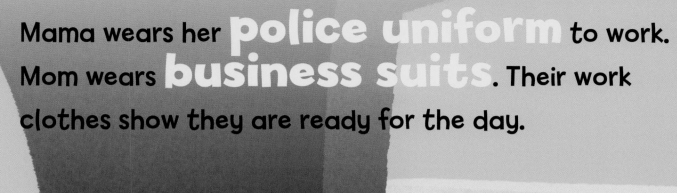

Mama wears her **police uniform** to work. Mom wears **business suits**. Their work clothes show they are ready for the day.

Clothes also show how people are alike.

"My **football jersey** lets other fans know if we cheer for the same team," my cousin Jordan says.

✓ Check! How can jerseys show people are alike?

9

CHAPTER 2

CLOTHES IN CULTURE

My sister, Lexi, goes to high school. She doesn't have to wear a uniform. Today she's wearing her **Chinese dress** since we are Chinese.

I wonder what the other students' clothes say about them.

Mama tells me about Amish people.

The Amish wear plain clothing
for religious reasons.

My friend Katie is Ojibwe. Ojibwe women and girls wear **jingle dresses** when dancing at powwows.

The dresses have metal cones on them that jingle when the dancers move.

My other friends wear other types of clothing. Ben is Jewish. He sometimes wears a cap called a **kippah**.

Sadia is Muslim. She wears a headscarf called a **hijab**.

✓ Check! What is Katie's special dress called?

17

CHANGING OUTFITS

My family dresses up for church.
It's a way of showing respect.

At home, I wear comfy clothes. I love my **bunny slippers**!

✓ Check! How do Chloe's home clothes differ from her church clothes?

BIG DECISION

Today is dress-up day.

21

LEARN ABOUT CLOTHING

Clothing can celebrate culture. Special clothing is a part of Ojibwe powwows. At powwows, the Ojibwe celebrate, pray, and socialize.

People may wear clothing for religious reasons. Some Muslim girls and women wear hijabs. Some Jewish people wear a small cap called a kippah.

Many schools around the world require students to wear uniforms. Uniforms can help students feel equal and welcomed.

People often show support for a sports team by wearing that team's jersey. People who are a part of a team wear the same jersey as their teammates.

People wear different clothing depending on their jobs. What do the adults in your life wear to work?

THINK ABOUT CLOTHING:
CRITICAL-THINKING AND TEXT FEATURE QUESTIONS

Does your family wear certain clothing for special occasions?

How are your friends' clothes similar to or different from yours?

Who is this book's illustrator?

Can you find the index in this book?

GLOSSARY

Amish: a Christian group that lives simply, dresses plainly, and focuses on their families and community

culture: the language, customs, and ideas of a group of people

Jewish: related to the religion called Judaism

Muslim: a follower of the religion of Islam

Ojibwe: indigenous people native to the region around the Great Lakes in the US and Canada

religious: belonging to a system of faith and worship

LEARN MORE

Bullard, Lisa. *A Special Invitation: All Kinds of Religions.* Minneapolis: Lerner Publications, 2022.

Lamothe, Matt. *This Is How We Do It: One Day in the Lives of Seven Kids from around the World.* San Francisco: Chronicle Books, 2017.

Murphy, Charles. *Clothing around the World.* New York: Gareth Stevens, 2017.

INDEX